"I CAN DO IT" DAY

by Louise McClenathan

Illustrated by Chris Demarest

HOUGHTON MIFFLIN COMPANY BOSTON

Atlanta Dallas Geneva, Illinois Palo Alto Princeton Toronto

It was "I Can Do It" Day.

"It's time to run," said Bear.

"Who can run?"

"I can!" said Rabbit.

"I can do it."

"I can't," said Frog.

"I can't run like a rabbit.

I wish I could, but I can't."

"One, two, three, GO!" said Bear.
"Run!"

Rabbit was the best.

"Now it's time to climb," said Bear.

"Who can climb?"

"I can!" said Cat.

"I can do it!"

"I can't," said Frog.

"I can't climb like a cat.

I wish I could, but I can't."

"One, two, three, GO!" said Bear.

"Climb!"

Cat was the best.

"Now it's time to fly," said Bear.

"Who can fly?"

"I can!" said Bird.

"I can do it!"

"I can't," said Frog.

"I can't fly like a bird.

I wish I could, but I can't."

"One, two, three, GO!" said Bear.
"Fly!"

Bird was the best.

"Now it's time to jump," said Bear.

"Who can jump?"

"I can!" said Frog.

"I can do it!"

"I can jump!" said Rabbit.

"I can, too!" said Cat.

"We can all jump!" said Bird.

13

"One, two, three, GO!" said Bear.

"Jump!"

Rabbit could jump.

Cat could jump.

Bird could jump.

But . . .

not like a frog.
Frog was the best!